1. Sick

Green words

fed up   bed   si<u>ck</u>   is   ba<u>ck</u>   in   am

Red words

I   my

I am in bed.

My tum is si<u>ck</u>.

My ba<u>ck</u> is bad.

I am fed up.

Questions to talk about

How is the person feeling?

What do you think is wrong with him?

Hold a sentence

_____

_____

2. Spin and slip

Green words	Red word
spin slip flip flop	I

I can spin.

I can slip.

I can flip.

I can flop.

I can spin, slip, flip and flop.

Questions to talk about

What do you think this person is doing?

Hold a sentence

_____

_____

3. Drink

Dr<u>ink</u> a cup of milk.

Dr<u>ink</u> a cup of pop.

Dr<u>ink</u> a cup of mud.

Questions to talk about

What do you like to drink?

Hold a sentence

_____

_____

4. Get up

Green words						Red word
sand	**skip**	**soft**	sun	run	wet	<u>th</u>e

Mum get up.

Dad get up.

Sam get up.

<u>Th</u>e sun is up.

Run on <u>the</u> sand.

Skip on <u>the</u> sand.

Soft wet sand.

Questions to talk about

How is the person feeling? How do you know?

Hold a sentence

_____

_____

5. The shop

Let's get hot <u>ch</u>ips from <u>the</u> <u>sh</u>op.

Let's get a can of pop from <u>the</u> <u>sh</u>op.

Hot <u>ch</u>ips and pop –

Mmmmm.

Questions to talk about

Where do you like to eat chips?

Hold a sentence

_____

_____

6. On a bench

Green words

ben<u>ch</u> grin sand

Red words

I th(e) m(y)

Challenge word

h<u>ea</u>d

I sit on a ben<u>ch</u>

in <u>the</u> sun on <u>the</u> sand,

a hat on my h<u>ea</u>d,

a grin on my lips.

Questions to talk about

Where is this girl sitting?

Hold a sentence

_____

_____

7. Puddle

Green words

splash kick jump grin sit then

Red word

the

Challenge word

puddle

Splash!

Kick the mud.

Run and then jump.

Sit in a puddle.

Grin in a puddle.

Questions to talk about

How is the child in the puddle feeling?

How do you know?

Hold a sentence

_____

_____

8. A black cab

A man in a flat cap gets in a bla<u>ck</u> cab.

A dog wi<u>th</u> lo<u>ng</u> legs gets in a bla<u>ck</u> cab.

A lad wi<u>th</u> red so<u>ck</u>s gets in a bla<u>ck</u> cab.

Questions to talk about

What is the man wearing?

What does the dog look like?

What is the lad wearing?

Hold a sentence

_____

_____

9. In bed

Green words	Red words	Challenge word
quick sick chin itch have scratch neck	I my	head

I am in bed. I am sick.

Scratch, scratch.

I have an itch on my chin.

I have an itch on my neck.

I have an itch on my head.

I have an itch on my legs.

I have an itch on my tum.

Get my mum. Quick!

Questions to talk about

Why is the boy in bed?

Hold a sentence

_____

_____

10. Red and pink fish

Red and p<u>in</u>k fi<u>sh</u>

P<u>in</u>k and bla<u>ck</u> fi<u>sh</u>

Fi<u>sh</u> wi<u>th</u> spots

Fi<u>sh</u> wi<u>th</u> dots

Flat fi<u>sh</u> wi<u>th</u> fins

Big flo<u>pp</u>y fi<u>sh</u>

Spla<u>sh</u>y spli<u>sh</u>y fi<u>sh</u>

Questions to talk about

Describe all the different fish.

Hold a sentence

_____

_____

11. I am black

Green words						Red word
shed	have	give	milk	live		I

I am bla<u>ck</u>.

I am big.

I ha<u>ve</u> a fat tum.

I gi<u>ve</u> milk.

I li<u>ve</u> in a <u>sh</u>ed.

I ha<u>ve</u> 4 legs.

I am a ...

Questions to talk about

What is the animal?

How do you know?

Hold a sentence

_____

_____

12. Shopping list

Green words

bun**ch**   cre**ss**   spri**ng** ro**ll**s   **sh**rimps   bran   ke**tch**up   e**gg**s

Challenge word

fi**zz**y

Red words

th(e)   o(f)

Questions to talk about

Fastest Finger (find the answer)

Which items on the list
could be eaten for:

- *breakfast?*

- *lunch?*

- *tea?*

Have a Think (explain why)

Which are the unhealthy foods
on the list?

Which are the healthy items
on the list?

Hold a sentence

a. _____

_____

b. _____

_____

Jan's shopping list

Jan is at <u>the</u> <u>sh</u>ops. <u>Th</u>is is Jan's <u>shopping</u> list:

<u>Shopping list</u>

a box of e<u>gg</u>s

red ke<u>tch</u>up

six buns

ten bags of crisps

fi<u>sh</u>

<u>sh</u>rimps

crab sti<u>ck</u>s

jam

a box of bran

fi<u>zz</u>y pop

milk

spri<u>ng</u> ro<u>ll</u>s

a bun<u>ch</u> of cre<u>ss</u>

nuts

lemons

plums

<u>ch</u>ips

(and a big box of <u>ch</u>ocs!)

13. Help!

Green words

flit	**gasp**	**mist**	bl<u>ink</u>	mo<u>ss</u>
sku<u>ll</u>	mo<u>th</u>	<u>wr</u>o<u>ng</u>		

Multi-syllabic word

cob|webs

Root words and suffixes

cla<u>nk</u> ➜ **cla<u>nking</u>**

cl<u>ink</u> ➜ cl<u>inking</u>

Red words

of I my no

Challenge words

cold o'clo<u>ck</u>

Questions to talk about

Fastest Finger (find the answer)

- *What can the narrator smell in his dream?*

- *What can he see?*

- *What does he touch?*

Have a Think (explain why)

- *Have you ever woken from a bad dream and not known where you are?*

- *What place could he be dreaming about?*

Hold a sentence

a. _____

_____

b. _____

_____

Help!

It's cold and damp.
Cobwebs brush my hands,
And moths flit past ...
No sun, just thick mist.
Wet, black moss.
Slugs
And a bad smell ...
This is wrong!
I blink.
Is that a *skull*?
A gust of wind.
A clinking and a clanking.
A hand grabs my leg!
"Help! Help!" I gasp.
I trip, and ...
"Get up, Tom!
It's 8 o'clock!"
Is that Mum?
Am I ... *in bed*?

14. Fed up

Questions to talk about

Fastest Finger (find the answer)

- *What is this girl fed up about?*

Have a Think (explain why)

- *How fed up do you think she is?*

- *Why do we not take her very seriously?*

- *What sort of things put you into a sulk?*

Hold a sentence

a. _____

_____

b. _____

_____

Fed up

I'm sitting on my bed
with the cat on my lap.
I'm fed up.

I'm fed up with Dad.
(I will not help
to wash the dishes.)

I'm fed up with Mum –
Helping is for wimps!

I'm fed up with posh Ella in my class,
And Josh, the lad I met at the swim club.
Josh is just sad.

I'm fed up with Miss Simms.
(Such a fuss!
It was just a stink bomb.)

And I'm fed up with egg and chips
for lunch.

I'm just sitting on my bed.
Sulking.
(Until I go to the swim club, that is.)

15. Packing

Green words
camp   list
Multi-syllabic words
ruck|sack   san|dals
Root words and suffixes
swim ➜ swi<u>mm</u>ing

Red words
to   all   of   ball

Challenge words
wa<u>sh</u>   f<u>or</u>

Questions to talk about

Fastest Finger (find the answer)

- *Can you list all the things that Dan packs to eat?*

- *Can you list all the things that Dan packs to wear?*

- *What are the things that will keep Dan amused?*

Have a Think (explain why)

- *Number the 5 most important things for the camp, in order of importance.*

Hold a sentence

a. _____

_____

b. _____

_____

Packing

Dan is o<u>ff</u> to Hi<u>ll</u> Crest Camp
wi<u>th</u> his pals Ben and Sam.
<u>Th</u>is is his list of <u>th</u>i<u>ng</u>s to pa<u>ck</u> in his ru<u>ck</u>sa<u>ck</u>:

<u>Packing list – Hill Crest Camp</u>
six tops
combats
vests
pants
bla<u>ck</u> swi<u>mm</u>i<u>ng</u> tru<u>n</u>ks
red swi<u>mm</u>i<u>ng</u> tru<u>n</u>ks
lots of so<u>ck</u>s
sandals
belt
cap
sungla<u>ss</u>es
lots of comics
ba<u>ll</u>
a pa<u>ck</u>et of Hobnobs
mints and gum
wa<u>sh</u>bag and wa<u>sh</u>i<u>ng</u> stu<u>ff</u>
ca<u>sh</u> <u>for</u> dri<u>n</u>ks and sna<u>ck</u>s
a big pot of stu<u>ff</u> <u>for</u> spots
and <u>th</u>at's <u>all</u>!

16. Simba

Green words

cub   ca<u>tch</u>   <u>qu</u>i<u>ck</u>   must   slim

Multi-syllabic words

a|cro<u>ss</u>   ze|bra

Root words and suffixes

run → ru<u>nn</u>i<u>ng</u>

tra<u>ck</u> → **tra<u>ck</u>i<u>ng</u>**

hunt → hunti<u>ng</u>

Red word

th<u>e</u>

Challenge words

<u>fo</u>r   dusty   bu<u>sh</u>es   f<u>oo</u>d

Questions to talk about

Fastest Finger (find the answer)

- *What animal is Simba?*

- *What is Simba tracking?*

Have a Think (explain why)

- *Is it day or night?*

- *How do we know the zebra is in danger?*

- *Do you think Simba will catch it?*

Hold a sentence

a. _____

_____

b. _____

_____

Simba

A big cat, running across long grass.
Hunting, tracking, zebra spotting …

This is Simba.
Simba has a cub.
Simba must hunt for food.

Trotting along a dusty track.
Hot sun.
Hunting, tracking …

Simba stops.
A twig snaps in the bushes.
Simba sniffs.
Zebra!
Quick, Simba!
Run!

Simba runs fast.
But the zebra runs fast as well,
on its long, slim legs.

Will Simba catch it?

17. Splash!

Green words

mast **fli<u>ck</u>** **spla<u>sh</u>** **<u>ch</u>est**

skin bru<u>sh</u>

Root words and suffixes

drift ➜ **drifti<u>ng</u>**

si<u>nk</u> ➜ **si<u>nk</u>i<u>ng</u>**

Red words

I of tall my me

Challenge words

cold salt gri<u>tt</u>y gold

di<u>zz</u>y <u>sh</u>ip<u>wr</u>eck

Questions to talk about

Fastest Finger (find the answer)

- *What can he taste?*

- *What can he feel?*

- *What is he imagining?*

Have a Think (explain why)

- *Where is this person?*

- *What sort of mood is he in?*

Hold a sentence

a. _____

_____

b. _____

_____

Splash!

I'm in.

I'm swimming.
Cold neck.
Cold hands.
Cold legs.
Gritty sand
and salt on my lips.

I'm sinking.
Soft plants brush my skin.
Fish flick past me
and crabs run off
as I kick my legs.

I'm swimming on my back,
thinking of a shipwreck,
a tall thin mast
a chest full of gold rings.

I'm on a flat rock.
Sun hot on my back.
I'm dizzy.
I'm drifting,
just drifting …

Hold a sentence

1.	I am fed up and sick.
2.	I can flip and flop.
3.	Can I drink a cup of pop?
4.	Run on the sand.
5.	Can I get hot chips?
6.	I sit on the hot bench.
7.	Run and jump in a puddle.
8.	I get in a black cab.
9.	I am sick in bed.
10.	A fish can swim.
11.	I am big and I live in a shed.